The Young Seducer: Marquis de Sade
Seventh and last part

Erika Sanders

Serie
The Young Seducer: Marquis de Sade Vol. 7

Synopsis

The young seducer: Marquis de Sade is a new series based on the life and works of the Marquis de Sade.

Alphonse is a young aristocrat who, being his father so protective and not letting him leave the castle walls where they live, in his adolescence he has not yet known the fruits of love.

With the arrival of an uncle, accompanied by his children, visiting the castle to see their father, everything will change.

The cousins, experts in the arts of love, begin to teach him everything that has been lost ...

This series is based on the compilation and study of anonymous erotic writings from the 19th century and adapted to the vision that the writer has of the life and work of the Marquis de Sade.

Note on the author:

Erika Sanders is an internationally known writer, translated into more than twenty languages, who signs her most erotic writings, away from her usual prose, with her maiden name.

Author's website:

https://www.instagram.com/erikaasanderss/

Contact E-Mail:

erikasanders98@gmail.com

Index:

THE YOUNG SEDUCTOR: MARQUIS DE SADE
SEVENTH PART
ERIKA SANDERS

CHAPTER 1

On the afternoon of the second day, I made great preparations for the event about to take place.

They served me a dinner so elegant that it would have tempted Epicurus himself.

All the women belonging to my harem were at the table and I served them so well, with high quality wine, that none, except Aysel, got up sober.

When I gave the signal for us to retreat to the bedroom, they moved, staggering, like many drunken sailors.

When we got to the room, we all undressed and I took Aysel in my arms.

I carried her to the center bed and threw her on her.

But fearing something that my potency was affected, since the African black slave had worn me out the other night, I ordered and drank a cup of my magic chocolate that I knew would allow me to go through all the intended acts as a conqueror.

I gave the order and all the girls surrounded the bed playing their instruments and singing a beautiful song that I had composed for the occasion.

With everything ready, I got on the bed, placed my slave in the best position, got between her thighs and passed a whip that was near the bed to one of the girls.

I grabbed my battering ram and struggled to force its way in.

The head is already in, the soft flesh gives way to my fierce thrusts.

I walk in, he screams in pain, but I don't stop.

It is music to my ears.

That tells me that I am about to reach the seat of bliss.

I push and push harder.

Everything makes me more passionate.

The spanking on my buttocks gives me double strength, and a fierce thrust from me sends me to the far end of his grotto.

At that very moment I watered the tender and bleeding deflowered flesh of my dear little slave with a stream of fiery sperm like never before a woman had received from a man.

I thought my cock and balls were dissolving in a constant stream of pearly liquid.

After resting for a moment on his chest, I discovered that my battering ram was ready for another round and fiercely pushed it back towards its opening.

Three times before she took me off, I wasted my body milk on her without asking her for any kind of favor.

She lay and moaned with pleasure and pain, and as I looked, I saw that she had hit and terribly hurt the entrance to the pleasure seat.

I picked her up and put her in a warm bath and after drying her I put her back to bed.

After giving him some wine and having some myself, I found that I was back in shape for another round.

Like a spring I put myself between her thighs.

I got into it, without much hard work anymore.

God of voluptuous love, what heat reigned in her body!

How deliciously his sweet flesh enveloped my strong rod!

A few thrusts and a few movements in and out awaken her to a sensation of pleasure.

He approaches me, he realizes the fever that runs through me.

Faster, faster, he lunges toward me to meet my ferocious thrusts as I lead my sparkling steed through his gap into the rich pasture.

She hugs me in her arms and throws her snowy thighs around my back, the rebounding of her butt pulling me out of her.

I feel like she's coming.

Oh my God, she comes, she comes!

The sperm now comes from her in a torrent.

Me too, I cum again!

A ... Great God! This is too much! I die! Oh! Oh!

And then release your spirit in a soft, gentle sigh.

My God, how voluptuous, how delicious is the Arab beauty! What heat it expels! With what fire, with what energy he met all my efforts to obtain and dispense pleasure! How deliciously it squeezed me when I was in it! How abundantly did she release the milk when the agony of pleasure invaded her!

We swim in a perfect sea of totally indescribable voluptuousness.

Man cannot imagine, the pen cannot describe it, it was an intoxication of delight: pleasure created in agony, inexpressible bliss, more exquisitely delicious than that enjoyed by the houris of Paradise when they are in the arms of true Muslims, or of the enjoyed by the spirits of the Champs Elysees.

CHAPTER 2

I felt considerably spent for a couple of days so I refrained from going back into my slave girls' caves of Venus until I got back on the ship to sail fairly on my projected cruise in search of love and beauty in the climates of America, where I expected the most exquisite pleasures from the ardent ladies of Cuba and the island of Hispaniola.

When arriving near Bordeaux I ordered to stop the navigation with the purpose of giving the sailors the opportunity to let off steam with some girls and so that Aysel and two other slaves, Mary and Fanny, would know my summer mansion, where they would stay to await my return from America.

In two days, everyone had already kidnapped a girl, so afterwards we left for Havana, since I had heard about the beauty of the women of the island.

The intention was to stop there long enough to get more slaves.

CHAPTER 3

After a few weeks of sailing, upon arriving in Havana, I took some rooms in one of the best hotels, giving orders to the Captain to keep the brig ready at all times so that I could quickly set sail at any time.

In the guest dining area I noticed a pretty and vivacious brunette, evidently an island resident.

His eyes were quite hidden under a mass of deep black hair that covered them with his shadow; but I could perceive that while I was at the table, she was looking at me continuously, and the moment my eyes met hers, she would suddenly drop her eyes to the plate or look in another direction.

From this, I augured favorably and considered the success to be true, thinking that I had made a conquest.

At night I attended the theater accompanied by the Captain, and the two well armed.

There I saw the lady in a box in the company of a couple of older gentlemen.

Who I took as her husband was an old-looking, ugly, and short-tempered guy.

I followed her to her hotel room to find out where she lived with the intention of winning her over.

CHAPTER 4

In the morning, when I showed up at his door, I was received by Mr. Don José Domínguez, the husband of Doña Juana, my lovely friend in the hotel dining room.

I told him that I was a gentleman of rank and fortune, traveling for pleasure with his own boat, and I invited him to the port to see the brig.

He accepted the invitation and when he arrived at the place he was very satisfied with the orderly cleanliness of everything on the deck and with the luxury that was displayed in the cabin accessories.

I ordered lunch to be made and packed with plenty of champagne so that when I got off the ship, I would be in high spirits.

Upon arriving at the hotel, he invited me to his apartment and introduced me to his wife and two other ladies we met with her.

I tried as hard as I could to make her notice in my expression that I had especially noticed her and was in awe of her charms.

After chatting for a short time, I retired to my room to dress for dinner.

There I wrote a letter to Doña Juana, declaring my passion for her and begging her to grant me an interview, since I read in her eyes that she herself was not unpleasant.

After dinner, I joined her and her husband and slipped my note into her hand, which she immediately hid in the folds of her dress.

Then I went to my room to wait for an answer, which I was sure would soon be sent.

I didn't have to wait long either, since in a couple of hours a black wench opened the door, poked her head out to determine if I was in the room, threw me a note, and closing the door without saying a word, she left.

I hastily picked up the note from the floor and upon opening it found my expectations confirmed!

She gave me an interview.

Her note said that her husband would go to his plantations the next day and that at three in the afternoon she would be alone taking her nap.

CHAPTER 5

The afternoon, the night, and the next morning passed me very slowly.

After eating, I retired to my room, leaving my watch on the table next to the bed and sat to look at the dial, watching the time go by, waiting anxiously.

But when the dial on the clock pointed to three o'clock, the same black wench opened the door again, poked her head out, looked around, and stepped back, leaving the door open.

I jumped up and followed her to her mistress's rooms.

There I found Doña Juana reclined in an elegant pose, relaxed, on a sofa.

She held out her hand in welcome, which I took and pressed against my lips.

She invited me to sit down and I settled on a stool next to her.

Taking her hand in mine, I revealed my passion for her, imploring her not to reject my love.

At first she pretended to be very surprised that I made a declaration of love to her and seemed even half angry.

But as I progressed with my love story and pressed her for a favorable response to the consuming passion, she seemed to give in.

And rising from her reclined position she left me room to sit next to her on the couch.

When I sat down next to her, I put an arm around her waist and pulled her into my body.

I begged her to grant me her love, even to leave her husband and go with me to some remote corner of the Earth where we could be far from here, to live our best years in the soft charm of love.

I told her that her husband was an old man with whom she could not enjoy life, and from whom a young woman like her could not receive those tender attentions that she required, and the soft and real pleasure that she could enjoy in the arms of a young man. devoted lover.

She sighed and lowered her head to his chest, saying that she had never known what it was like to receive, from her husband, those delicious and tender pleasures that he had just told her about.

That from the moment their marriage occurred to the present moment, all his time was busy drinking and playing games.

That he left her to have the best fun he could around the house, and he was so jealous that he would never let her go out, except in his company.

She sighed again and wished heaven had given her a man like me before her marriage.

I don't know how it happened, but when she stopped talking, I suddenly discovered that one of my hands had parted the front of her dress and was slipping under her nightgown.

So, not receiving displeasure from her, I began to run my hand over one of her large, hard breasts, and my lips pressed on hers.

My lean against her had moved her sensibly back until, unintentionally, her head was already resting on the sofa cushion and I was lying on top of her.

Meanwhile, I assured him of eternal love and constancy and begged him to allow me to give him convincing proof of my tenderness and affection.

Also that she let me convince her that until now she had experienced the mere shadow of the ecstatic pleasure of love, but that, if she allowed me, I would give her the real substance and even an excess of those pleasures of which I felt convinced that she did not. she had received more than a pinch from her husband.

So I gradually lifted her clothes, until my hand rested on a large, firm, meaty thigh.

Joan had closed her eyes, her head hanging to one side, her lips slightly parted, and her chest rising and falling rapidly from the rapid pulses of blood caused by her fierce, loving desires.

I lifted her nightgown even higher until a large lock of long black hair came into view.

Then I unbuttoned my pants and, with a little force, parted her legs and crawled between her thighs.

Separating the vaginal lips with my fingers, I inserted the head of my love engine, and in a few moments we were both panting in the middle of the most exquisite transports of love.

After cumming, I lay down exhausted on her chest while she remained motionless beneath me.

I found that my stiffness had barely lessened, and from the short strokes and jerks of the head of my cock, I knew that it was once again ready for action, and impatient for the battle to begin again.

So I started to move inside her again.

"Beautiful creature," I yelled, "what delicious sensations! What a pleasure! My God!" I said, "You were almost a virgin. How deliciously tight your sweet flesh grips my rod!"

Her arms were tight around my neck, her thighs around my back, her wet pink lips glued to mine.

Our tongues met.

With what vivacity, with what voluptuousness he moves towards me, giving me energetic arches for my thrusts.

From the increasing movement of her butt I felt that again she was about to dissolve in bliss.

I felt it too.

"Ah, my God! Oh, what a pleasure! I come again. Like this, dear, love, don't stop now: What joy, what love, what unbearable happiness!"

And similar things the pretty black girl told me while I fucked her, swimming in a sea of pleasure, in a perfect agony of bliss.

When we recovered from our delirium, I got up, lowered her clothes slowly over her legs, and pressed her to my side.

Planting a soft kiss on her pursed lips, I crossed her in my arms and asked her how she liked reality after being fed for over a year with the mere shadow of that delicious substance that she had just tasted.

The answer was a kiss that sent an emotion of pleasure through all the veins.

"Oh dear, this is nothing you would enjoy if you joined your fortune with mine and traveled with me to France. Then we would live a life full of love and pleasure like the one you just tried. Our whole life would be nothing more than love and pleasure, morning, noon and night would be love, all love. There should be nothing around us but love, and nothing but pleasure! "

Joan rang a small bell and the same ebony girl entered who had twice placed her head in and out of my bedroom door.

His mistress told him to bring a lunch, and he soon returned with an elegant cold meal and delicious wine.

After eating and drinking, we turned our attention back to love.

Getting up from the chair, I carried her to the sofa and, pulling her on my knees, I removed her dress.

I loosened the strings of her bodice to play with her breasts, which were really beautiful, big and firm, and with two nipples, strawberry-shaped, very tempting.

My partner was not idle either, since while I was engaged taking off her clothes and playing with her breasts, she unbuttoned my pants and pulled out my cock, which I admired and played around, covering and uncovering the foreskin until it brought it to a state very beautiful erection.

I lifted her to her feet and letting her clothes slide on the floor, she stood with all her beauty naked in front of me.

What charms, what beauties delighted my eyes and my lips as I turned it round and round.

Her round soft belly, her plump butt and then her beloved cleft, that masterpiece of beauty, how she had hugged my cock before.

And the kisses she lavished on her, all of which she paid me with interest.

He kneels on the floor between my legs.

She strokes my cock, presses it against her lips.

He pouts and she puts my big red head between them.

I push forward a little, enter her mouth, she sucks on me, her soft tongue rolling it over and over.

She continues to tickle me with her tongue.

Feeling that if she continues like this I will come right away, I step back and take her out of her mouth.

She wants to put it in her mouth again.

I lay her on the floor with the cushions under her buttocks.

I continue to put my head between her thighs, with my cock and balls hanging over her face.

Again she takes it to her mouth, while I put my tongue between her pussy lips and rub her clit with it.

The movement of her butt increases!

I realize that he is about to come and suddenly I get up, I sit on the sofa.

She sits up behind me, jumps on the couch, her pussy touching my face, her arms tightly around my neck.

He slowly dropped his butt, until it touched the head of my cock.

I direct it correctly and she impales herself on my cock.

A few movements and I irrigate her completely with my milk while she also pays her own homage to the God of Love with her nectar on my cock.

When he rose from me, the combined sperm of both fell from his salacious cleft in great drops on me, testifying to the abundant measure with which nature had endowed us both with the elixir of life.

CHAPTER 6

In the evening, she sent her maid to order that her supper be delivered to her rooms, and, after suppering in silence, we retired to bed and I spent the most pleasant night I have ever had with any woman.

Her husband returned the next day, but I found the opportunity to visit his wife in the evening and we renewed for a short time the transportation that we had enjoyed the day before.

A few days later, her husband had invited a party of six pairs of young ladies and the same number of young men to visit his wife and have dinner with them.

I was also invited.

Immediately after receiving the invitation, I sent a message to the Captain to expedite the necessary preparations so that he would be ready to sail at any time.

I joined the party for dinner and found that three of the invited girls were pretty but the other three were even prettier, all black.

After dinner was over, I invited the group to visit my yacht for an evening excursion with me.

My lover's husband was greatly exaggerated in his praise for the beauty of the yacht and the rich and elegant way it was prepared and joined his requests with mine.

With his consent, we ordered carriages and headed to where the yacht was anchored.

Climbing aboard, we sailed to the port and toured the island.

After we stopped seeing the city, I took the Captain aside and told him that towards the evening I wanted him to take the brig to shore; and that he intended to have the seven men caught, put them in a boat, and flee with the women.

I told him to go and talk to the crew about the matter and to be ready to obey my signal.

A little before dark, we were sailing near the coast through a place where there were no visible plantations.

I had ordered some ropes to be scattered on the main deck and I ordered the Captain to send the sailors to collect it.

Sixteen hardcore sailors came astern and suddenly seized the men and bound their arms and legs.

Then I told them what I intended to do, ordering some of the sailors to accompany the women downstairs.

I did not listen to the execrations and pleas of the men for the women who were their wives, but I made them get into a boat to send them ashore.

There they were untied and left.

The boat returned to the brig and we set sail for France.

CHAPTER 7

The girls did nothing but sob and cry for a day or two, but they soon calmed down.

Immediately after landing in Bordeaux, I entered the house and, taking Aysel, Mary, and Fanny out of their rooms, I introduced them to the new company of pretty Cuban women.

When dinner was served, all the Cuban women refused to sit at the table and eat.

But I told them that if they did not comply with all my wishes, I would hand them over to the sailors to use as they chose.

This had its quick effect on them and they sat down at the table.

I rang the bell and two of the most beautiful women we took in Bordeaux who belonged to the sailors came in completely naked.

I had ordered them to wait for my signal to make coffee.

The Cuban girls were about to get up, but with a dry scream, I threatened them.

The first ones to get up should spend the night with the men.

This had an effect on them and they stayed still.

While the servants were preparing the coffee, I got up and went to the end table as if to look for something, but in reality I poured a few drops of a certain liquid into each cup of coffee.

The amount put into each cup was enough to ignite the licentious and loving desires of any woman.

They all drank their coffee and in about half an hour the effect was very visible.

All the shyness of modesty was gone and their gazes languished excitedly, joking about the nakedness of the servant girls.

Whenever they were within reach of them, they pinched or spanked them.

The effect produced by the drug that I put in the coffee was that great.

When dinner was over and the tables were cleared, I began to play and fight with them.

Roll them on the ground and play a thousand love tricks on them that paid with interest: throwing me to the ground, falling on me.

While receiving a kiss from one of them, she would squeeze a thin breast and slide her other hand over one thigh, or slip one hand under a petticoat and grasp a large calf or a well-shaped knee with the other.

I ordered a very good quality wine to be brought, well seasoned with the love potion.

I invited them to the wine that they drank very happily and in a couple of hours all reserve and modesty had left them.

I took the Doña, the wife I had seduced in the hotel and whose husband had left ashore with the others, to one side and invited her to enter one of the rooms with me.

Then I asked her if she could forgive me for stealing her from her old cuckold husband.

He threw himself into my arms and with a fervent hug and kiss sealed my forgiveness with his lips.

Then I asked her to undress and told her that I would be back with her in a moment.

I went out, gave Mary an order, and returned, finding my lover naked in just her nightgown.

I undressed and, as I took off her nightgown, I gave her a kiss, I ran it over her head and we were both naked.

I opened the bedroom door and walked her into the girls' room.

Juana had already gotten drunk just like the girls who had come on board with her.

With what shouts of laughter they welcomed us, tickling us, pinching us, slapping us against each other, grabbing my genitals and pulling the hair that surpassed my lover's slit, caressing our naked behinds, throwing us on the ground one on top of the other, etc.,

While I caught them, I lifted their petticoats, pinched their glutes, shook the head of my huge cock against the lips of their little hairy slits, forced it against their hands and made them play with my cock.

I caught one and with the help of Aysel and my lover we soon undressed her, handing her clothes over to Mary, who had been ordered, along with Aysel, to have their clothes removed earlier, which is why they were just as naked as I was.

Little by little we were catching all the black girls, and in a few minutes we had completely undressed them all.

Oh then what loving and unbridled tricks we play sportingly together.

They tickled my big balls, they played with my penis and rubbed it, I molded their beautiful tits and with the tip of my finger I tickled all their pussies.

A little black devil that looked like the youngest of the group made me cum.

How fun this was for the rest of us, to later watch her rest her head on my shoulder, spread her thighs so I could stick my fingers in and gasp her exclamations of delight.

Her ohs and ahs, as she gave me her generous fluid that ran through my fingers and moistened my entire hand.

While I was with my finger rubbing the dear girl, Juana had squatted between my legs and had taken my cock in her mouth and was sucking me in that way as sweet as she did in Cuba.

I didn't notice it until the luscious creature that was leaning on my shoulder had finished coming.

But I felt like I was about to come too, but as I tried to pull my penis out of her mouth, she squeezed my buttocks with her hands and pressed me against her mouth, until my balls hit her chin and neck.

I exclaimed:

"My God! Let him go. I'm going to come!"

But instead of doing it, she hugged me even more and tickled the head of my cock more and more.

The crisis took hold of me, the short, convulsive jerks of my butt announcing that the fluid is coming.

"I'm cumming; here it is. Oh my God! What a pleasure! How exquisite! What bliss! Oh, God! Faster! Oh, what bliss! Heavenly joy! I am cumming inside your mouth ",

After finishing with all my torrent in his mouth I fell to the ground quite passed out from excess of pleasure.

My flesh trembled and danced, my whole body was in motion, as if attacked with the infernal dance.

Never, no, never in the world had a man experienced such exquisite pleasure and so full of women.

Never before has a man experienced such voluptuous pleasure.

There has never been such a heavenly, ecstatic bliss imparted to a man by a woman, as the one I received from my lover as he let my pearly liquid flow into his mouth.

Never has the most exquisite suction and friction of a pussy produced the same amount of ecstasy as intense as I felt when I came inside her mouth.

When the pearly liquid gushed out of me, he placed his tongue over my head, turning it over and over again, giving me feelings of bliss so delicious it made me feel convulsions of pleasure.

CHAPTER 8

It was some time before I recovered, and then it was through the teasing and tickling of my lovely torturers.

There was an orgy between the girls on the floor of the chamber but I already told them that it was late, and turning off the lights, we went to bed.

I was in Juana's arms and soon I paid her for the pleasure she had given me just before.

Three times I passed the warm and generous fluid that acts so powerfully on women in the most secret recesses of her slit, and then I composed myself to sleep.

After sleeping what must have been about two hours, I woke up to the feeling that someone was rubbing and playing with my member, which was already prepared for battle.

I discovered that it was Juana, who had her butt glued to the crook of my thighs and she was rubbing the head of my penis against her butt.

I wet him from time to time and the slide between his fat buttocks caused a very pleasant tingling sensation that permeated my entire body system.

Desiring to aid her in her intentions, even pretending to be asleep, I assisted her in whatever way I could in regards to position, etc.

But then I closed my arms around his waist and one thigh, which I raised slightly.

"Oh," he said, "you're awake and want more pleasure!"

I didn't respond and guided my cock's head into her tight little hole.

I pushed forward but he couldn't penetrate.

With my fingers I moistened the head with saliva and repositioned it, but could not overcome the entrance to the narrow hole.

Since it was an awkward position to lie down, I put her on her belly, placing a cushion under her to lift her ass up high.

I spread her thighs, got between them and so, again, I tried the rear entrance.

I forced my member to enter.

She squirmed and writhed gasping with pleasure she could barely contain.

Her movements and the luscious contractions of her ass brought me a copious discharge of electrical fluid that I injected into her.

"Oh God!" she exclaimed, "What a pleasure I feel that it invades me! How hot it is, my dear love! Again, and faster, now I also come; it is already coming out of me. My God! It is heaven! What pleasure! Ah, what a delicious pleasure!"

The words died on his lips.

Meanwhile, he was already fucking her in her slit again and he was rubbing her clit at the same time, getting her double the pleasure.

Here was an entirely new source of pleasure which was opened to me by the debauchery of my new lover.

I had already enjoyed her in three different places, and I discovered that she had penetrated the deepest recesses of my being, creating a sensation there that I felt could never be erased by any other woman.

It was a luxury to see the wild and stunned amazement of the lovely girls who surrounded us to find themselves lying with us, completely naked.

And, somehow, his arousal increased, I dare say, when he saw me on top of Juana, giving her ass again with her insatiable appetite for a delicious awakening, like the one provided by me this morning, which she sucked with great delight. .

But when I finished depositing my hot milk on my lovely Juana's ass, all the Cuban women jumped in search of her clothes or something to hide their nakedness, but to no avail; No clothes were seen, since they were kept under lock and key.

The dazzling little creature in whose arms she had spent the night almost laughed out loud at witnessing the girls' stupid stupor and began to criticize them, telling them everything that had happened during the night, remembering all their follies and extravagances.

She had been reluctant at first and tried to explain them to face their good luck, as she said, with strength, describing all the pleasure she had received from me during the night and begging them to submit to whatever I wanted with good grace as it would be the best for them.

Then I spoke to them, telling them where the resistance made by them would lead them, which would return them to the fierce wishes of ordinary sailors; but on the contrary, if they acted as I wanted, everything should go well with them.

As soon as they had just formed the slightest wish, it would be fulfilled instantly.

The finest attentions should be paid to them, and I ended by telling them of the life of luxury and wonderful love that they would lead with me, and on the contrary, the terrible life they would pass if they remained reluctant and forced me to turn them away from the brutal lusts of the sailors.

This had a considerable effect on them, as he could see fear and horror clearly depicted on their faces.

Then I rang a bell to call a servant and told her to bring me a bottle of wine, telling the girl where to get it.

When she brought it, I filled the glasses and asked the black girls, who were huddled together in the corner, to come and have a glass each.

They didn't move, and with a frown, I ordered them to come drink.

They approached the table and drank the wine.

I told them to sit on the couch while they served breakfast.

There were four of us sitting on a couch and I tried to get down on her knees, but they all jumped up and ran into a corner.

I decided to terrorize them immediately, so that they would be perfectly subordinate to my wishes.

Calling a servant, I sent her to call my companion, one who was officiating as my valet.

When he entered the chamber, I ordered the girls to return to their places on the couch, which they did shaking.

Then I told the partner to get hold of the first one to try to move, drag it to the deck of the ship and give it to the sailors.

I walked over to them and sat on one of them for a moment.

Liego lay on my back, with my face towards theirs.

The one on whose thighs my feet rested, I asked her to spread her legs and with my toes I tickled the lips of her bushy slit.

The one on whose thighs my head rested I also made her spread her legs so I could drop my right arm between them.

Then I rubbed her clit occasionally with my little finger, tickling her just inside her lips; she began to squirm on the couch.

The other two girls my glutes and thighs rested on began to play with me, one with my balls and the other with the baton.

At breakfast he had put enough of the aphrodisiac tincture in the younger and prettier girl's cup to make her lustful desires show quite strongly.

After we finished breakfast, I took this girl to a couch and put her on her knees, and when the drug started to take effect on her, I took all the freedoms I wanted with her, kissing and sucking on her pretty lips, her nipples, her breasts, manipulating her buttocks, rubbing her clit, lifting my big machine between her thighs and rubbing her pussy lips, until I felt able to make an entrance anywhere, no matter how small it was.

Meanwhile, she held me in her arms, kissing me back, rubbing and screwing her butt on my thighs, giving evidence of the raging fever that was consuming that part of her.

Her companions, none of whom had seen me pour the tincture into their coffee, considered her maneuvers with me with perfect amazement; without thinking that each one would do the same before more than two days passed.

I put a cushion and a pillow on the sofa to support her properly on her head and belly, and as I laid the little imp on her stomach, I spread her legs wide and stood between them.

She willingly helped me to fix it well, so that everything would work better.

Mary and Aysel came to act as pilots to steer my noble ship to the backport of love.

The entrance to the refuge was very narrow, which made the way difficult until Doña Juana ran towards me and hit me hard on the bare buttocks which took me inside to the hilt, making the delicious creature I was anally deflowering scream of pain.

Milk flowed from her and sperm from me, mixing deliciously.

Resting for a moment, I restarted the delicious run and soon had the joy of knowing that the dear girl was reaching the peak of human enjoyment while at the same time drowning my senses in another discharge of that peculiar fluid that drowns one in such ecstasy. .

I served three others in the same way, before the end of the day, removing those unpleasant reactions, which are of no use to a woman, and which I especially like to bend.

I forced one of them to give up her anal virginity without the help of the tincture and without taking her senses.

Oh! it was bliss, doubly refined, with its fierce struggles to free itself from my lascivious embraces.

How sweetly musical to my ears were his cries of anguish and shame.

With what transport I forced her to give up her sweet body to my ferocious desires.

How dazzling was the pleasure I felt in tearing open the tender exterior works, the interior doors, the bastions, everything.

And finally, even though she kept fighting and screaming, I made her bow fully to enter the temple of Venus itself.

Gods! It was such an exquisitely delicious fucking that it was half an hour before I recovered enough to re-enter Venus's little grotto, the path I had just enjoyed.

Lovely creature!

On three occasions I experienced in his arms that fierce pleasure of transport that intoxicates the soul and drowns the mind in those voluptuous ecstasies that can only be experienced in the close embrace of the two sexes.

CHAPTER 9

Refraining from living with any of the girls for a couple of days, I felt my strength renewed and invigorated, and on the fifth day later brought to France, I forced the rear entrance of the other three that were missing.

They fought hard to avoid it, but once they lost their anal virginity, which was so guarded, they entered all my whims and pleasures with the passion and ardor that characterizes females of Spanish blood.

Once the Rubicon was crossed, they became the biggest libertines I have ever come across.

They surrounded me day and night, trying by all means in their power to keep my cock in a constant state of erection.

They lay me on the ground completely naked, like them.

They were fighting precisely for the possession of my genitals.

One gently squeezed my balls, while another played with my penis, which she did with the gentle friction of her soft and delicate hand to achieve an erection.

Then she would rush over to me and devour the rich morsel, savoring it with those exquisite internal contractions and squeezes that at that moment when women are about to come make the act of intercourse so exquisitely delicious.

So when one was mounted on me, the other dear creatures showed all the fire of their Spanish lust.

Two of them seized my hands with their slit, one in each and, by running my fingers through their salacious slits, with the friction with my fingers of the rigid red tips, they obtained an appearance of the pleasure that their lucky rival was enjoying. and receiving from the horn that sprouted from the bottom of my belly and that she had impaled on her little pussy.

Juana was rushing into the arms of the Arab Aysel, whom she had liked very much.

Lying on the floor hugging each other, they rubbed and squeezed each other's breasts, sucked on each other's nipples, and stuck their tongues in each other's pussy.

The hands of each played and tangled in the thick hair that shadowed above the other's slit.

The fingers slid down, entered the sacred grotto, and then, sliding as far as they could, the arousal began.

And with the finger of the other hand, at the same time, they rubbed the clitoris, which soon brought them to that delicious state of annihilation that makes the soul dissolve in a sea of bliss.

At other times they would seize the languishing Fanny, who still retained her maidenhead, but was very eager to get rid of, and threw her on the sofa or on the floor.

And while Aysel was squeezing or sucking her breasts, squeezing hers, with her beautiful tits in her mouth, kissing and sucking her pink lips, and sticking her tongue in her mouth, Juana was between her thighs, rubbing her clit with her fingers and with your tongue between your lips.

Thus he excited her pussy to give her the most delicious pleasure.

Dear Fanny would come, pouring the liquor of which she possessed in abundance, on Aysel's tongue, in the middle of sighs, long and deep.

Nor were her hands idle, because those who were giving her pleasure were not forgetting themselves.

They forced their hands so that each one went to the hot oven of the other two and sent a flow of liquid that moistened Fanny's hands everywhere.

So, would they do everything possible to get Fanny those pleasures that around her they continually received from me, but of which I had still deprived her?

But it didn't take long for the day to come when what all maidens yearn to happen, to get rid of their virginity.

Giving myself a day off, I lay in the chamber alone on a mattress.

The girls always made their beds on the floor and we slept together.

After having been asleep for some time, I woke up to the feeling that someone was playing with my private parts.

Juana and Aysel lay on either side of me, their heads resting on my thighs.

Juana had taken that piece of meat that she liked so much in her mouth and was tickling it with her tongue.

The other was feeling and playing with the curious bag that hung between my thighs, gently rubbing and squeezing the balls.

My machine stood proudly like a mast, its red head glowing in the dark.

"Come on," said Juana, "Aysel has lived for five days in the shadow of the substance the other girls have been so gorging on, and it's only fair that you reward her for starving, while others have lived in abundance. Come, stand up! Your cock is in good condition. You must spend tonight with her and me because I haven't partaken of meat for some time. "

I put Aysel on her back and getting between her legs, I inserted my cock into her parts.

The moment he felt his head inside the recesses of her pussy, his belly began to move.

I worked hard on her for a while, withholding my own liquor as long as possible to give her the most pleasure possible, and she came three times in the process.

Just as she was finishing her third orgasm on my cock, I reached out and injected her with my abundant retained seed into her uterus.

I got out of her, and lay down between the two of them.

Without giving me time to rest, Juana began to play with my ram, which she hugged, pressing it against her breasts, squeezing it between them, pressing it against her cheeks, gently rubbing it with her hand and taking his uncovered head between her lips, gently biting and tickling him with the end of his tongue.

Then, stopping until he sank on my still wrinkled cock, he took it and took it whole to his mouth, and to his exquisite palate.

His sucking and tickling brought her back to life, proudly raising her head to her little lips that could barely encompass her anymore.

I laid her on her belly, placing a pillow under her lower body, and then I entered her rear hole.

I put my left hand under her thighs and inserted my fingers into her pussy, keeping them stiff, as I worked on her anus.

The movements of her ass, caused by the fall of my thighs against her butt, made her rub on my fingers.

Thus she enjoyed a double pleasure.

Nor was Aysel left without sharing this beautiful scene.

She had lain down with her belly on my chest, her bush and cleft rubbing against my side, her right thigh on my head.

Pulling her close to me, I kissed her pussy lips.

I tickled her clitoris with my tongue, put it between my lips and excited her so deliciously with them that she vanished with pleasure, at the same time that Juana was losing her sense towards the convulsive transports in which my double rub had thrown her. .

After this performance ended, we were completely exhausted in each other's arms for about two hours, at the end of which I began to feel somewhat revived.

CHAPTER 10

While we slept together, Juana had been describing to Aysel the intense pleasure she had enjoyed when I penetrated her rear hole, and the idea prevailed over her to force me to rub her in the same way.

So I had her lay her head between my thighs to play with my little thing and wake her up to a new life.

The beautiful, delicate and voluptuous Aysel took my cock in her mouth and by the tickle of her tongue and the sucking she gave it, she soon made him stand more beautifully upright, after which she let him go.

I soon put her in a convenient position for the attack, which was to strip her of her anal maidenhood, and she was perfectly willing to surrender immediately.

I put her on her right side, partially lying on her back.

Then I lay down on her left side and prepared to enter her.

Juana had lain in front of Aysel.

Her pussy touching her face and her head between her partner's thighs.

Juana raised the head of my enormous machine to her mouth, which she moistened well with saliva and then guided her to her destination.

But the place was so small that I made many attempts before I could penetrate it.

I finally felt him enter.

I pushed slowly and steadily, and in the end I felt it was impossible to go any further.

Aysel squirmed and squirmed so much after getting into her that I could barely stay on top of her.

Juana had put the fingers of her right hand in the cunt of the beautiful creature I was caressing, and the movements of her back as we worked together made her rub against them.

At the same time, Aysel put her own arms around Juana's buttocks, and bringing the slit close to her mouth, she put her tongue in it and rubbed it so well in this way that Juana came before either of us, wetting the tongue and lips of the beautiful Arab with the pearly drops of Juana's nectar.

The crisis now took hold of me.

At the same moment, the brush of Juana's fingers made Aysel come at the same time that I was squirting a jet of boiling sperm into her rectum.

"Ah, dear sir, have mercy on me! I feel it here inside me! Me too! Oh my God! I'm coming! Oh dear, what a pleasure. I die, I come again, again! I'm coming!"

Aysel relaxed the convulsive grip she had on Juana's rear.

Her flesh shuddered and danced and she lay convulsed with pleasure, as the gods never dreamed of.

CHAPTER 11

After another week in Bordeaux, we all got back on the ship and headed for the castle.

We reached the shore and anchored in the small stream.

We immediately went ashore, and taking the women with me, we went to the castle.

Heavens! What a welcome I received.

How lively, wild and lustful girls flocked to each other and what hugs they greeted me with.

I was quite eaten by the hungry creatures that huddled to hug me.

And, The Loving Rose! Ah, my dear Catherine, when I held you in my arms and received your fiery kisses, what emotion they sent me throughout my body.

And you, beautiful Odette, how your little heart beat when I pressed your chest against mine; what fire shone in your languid black eyes when you put one of my hands in your pussy and yours in my, already rigid, big cock.

Then came Giselle, the delicate Giselle with fair skin and blue eyes.

With what fierce delight she leaped forward, light as a fiery gazelle, into my arms.

What lustful fires flickered in his narrowed eyes.

His lips meet mine, they are glued.

She forces my mouth open, her tongue meeting mine.

She rubs her pussy lips against my thigh, closes her arms tightly, her breasts rise and swell in rapid succession, she wiggles her butt, her ass jerks convulsively and says, "Oh, oh, God!" and slipping into my arms he falls to the ground.

There, at the other end of the room, I see Brigitte enter.

Brigitte, that same goddess of voluptuous beauty.

She has heard of my arrival.

She walks towards me, completely naked except for a pink gauze around her waist.

I'm already naked too, because the girls had stripped me of all my clothes when I entered the room.

My cock is hard and stiff, standing upright against my belly.

Brigitte sees him, fixes her eyes on him and remains perfectly still, fascinated by the enchanting sight.

I fly towards her, I take her in my arms, her emotions dominate her, she lies down on her back, she drags me with her.

When I fall, his legs part and I fall between them, and five times he came before he got out from under me.

When he got up, what a glow flashed in his eyes.

His gait was light and springy like a fawn's.

When I rose from my fall with the charming Brigitte, I met the gaze of the licentious African, who was advancing towards me, holding in her hand a glass of wine.

She was perfectly naked and twisted and her thighs were screwed.

I meet her, accept the glass, and drink the wine.

The moment I drank it, I knew it was mixed with the tincture to excite and create love propensities.

All the lovely creatures I just named gathered around me.

They hugged me everywhere.

Some a leg and a thigh; others hung around my neck; some seized my hands with which they rubbed.

One sits on the floor between my legs and playfully squeezes my balls and strokes my cock one more time.

The luscious Shaira has her arms crossed around my neck and I am about to pierce her with my erection, but Fanny steps forward and asks for her claim on behalf of her little maiden, who is consuming her with a burning fever.

I take her in my arms and lay her down, falling over her.

One of the girls rushes to place a cushion under her butt and then guides the dart into her sheath.

I pushed and pushed, and one of the girls, giving me a couple of hard slaps on my butt, brought me up to the hilt and the sweet girl immediately absorbed the delicious liquor she had been waiting for.

The wine I had drunk contained so much tincture that my big cock continued to stand even after pouring all its liquor into Fanny's uterus.

Then, the African was placed for a good cumshot inside her entered for a good caress.

He came three times while he was inside her.

Brigitte, Odette, and Giselle came in turn; each received an exquisite blast of fiery liquor.

Then I went to bathe, taking only four of the girls: Brigitte, Rose, Odette, and Giselle.

While I was in the bathroom, twice more I screwed Giselle and Odette, and then I fired them to their apartments, keeping the other two.

Lunch was brought to the bathroom and, deciding to sacrifice myself for the lustful desires of my two adorable lovers, I drank more wine containing the tincture.

Enough to allow me to give the two who were with me as much milk broth as they could drink during the night.

After staying in the bathroom for a couple of hours, we went out and went to the bedrooms.

I led them into the room with the bed in the center of the room and, dropping the curtains, jumped onto the bed.

The two girls followed me and I will bury myself to the extreme in Rose's fiery furnace.

Four times this gentle creature let out her milk and it came out so profusely that the sheet under her butt was completely wet.

In turn, Brigitte took and stuffed her greedy little pussy with my mouthful.

So I spent the night, first fucking one and then the other, until they were completely spent and were exhausted with the delicious fuck I had given them.

CHAPTER 12

So I decided to stop looking for more maidens to kidnap and I gave myself to the dear girls I already owned, whom I could not find more beautiful, more voluptuous or more dedicated to my capricious pleasures.

I live happily surrounded by the sweet creatures, but now I hear someone calling me from my private bed.

I am in good condition, I have abstained for three days.

I go swiftly towards her, I jump into her arms and I drown in a sea of happiness, in the arms of La Rosa Amorosa.

END OF THE SAGA

51

THE VOYEUR HUSBAND
BY
ERIKA SANDERS

This is the first time we have planned this.

You, my love, want me to fuck with a stranger to see how I enjoy with another and penetrate me later.

I can't deny you any whims and you organized it last week.

I arrived at the five-star hotel where you had reserved a room for me, a hotel specifically chosen in a residential part of a big city where neither of us live.

It was a very comfortable junior suite, where I settled down at ease.

You had asked me to come down to dinner alone in the dining room afterwards, you were sure there would be some unknown executive, preferably a foreigner, dining there.

I remembered one of your stories in a hotel in Paris, where you were just talking to the sommelier, and I thought it was a good inspiration.

I dressed very carefully, I looked like a serious executive who was dining alone.

I downloaded a book to read, and decided that I would only speak English to see that I was fishing.

I sat at a table in the corner, ordered a very dry sherry, and began to read my book.

When they started bringing my food, I saw out of the corner of my eye that there were two good-looking executives, one tall and one short, who had removed their ties and were watching from the bar.

They looked at me a lot, until when I looked at them with a smile they raised their glasses to my health.

I laughed and motioned for them to come closer.

I saw that at the back of the lobby you had come and sat hiding behind an economics newspaper at a point where you could see me.

The men motioned to me that later, they sat down to dinner and I continued with my dinner and my book, without purposely looking at them again.

When I finished, I signed, left a tip, and got up to leave.

Then one of them, the shorter one, who had a little belly hidden in a well-cut double-breasted suit and a malicious smile, approached me.

"Hi there, my friend and I would like to invite you for a drink ..." he said.

"Thank you very much, but I am exhausted," I replied with a smirk.

"It will be a quick drink, don't worry," he replied

"Ok then. I will wait for you at the bar."

Without looking again, I went to the bar and ordered a low-sugar mojito, which the bartender made for me in a minute.

How long it took them to arrive and sit next to me.

"Hi again", I said with a small smile

They introduced themselves, they were both Canadians, they had come on business and were going back to Vancouver the next day.

I told them that my name was Jeane and that I was an interpreter.

We started talking about salmon and universities, and we finished confidences.

The two married, with almost college kids, the two close friends.

I only commented that I was married, without children, living in London and that I was working these days in this city.

I looked at them sympathetically, cordially ... and suggested they come and have another drink in my suite, if they wanted.

They looked at each other with sweet eyes and said yes on the spot.

The three of us went up in the elevator, and I still did not make the slightest movement towards them. But they each stood to one side and took my arm. I laughed and when I got out of the elevator I took them to my room. I had left it ready ... and as soon as I entered, I turned on the lights that were dimmed to give low light, and the music from my computer that I had left running was heard. Café del Mar, the one that relaxes you ...

I told them to take off their jacket and use my minibar, which was curiously in my room.

I had left the bed open, as if I had just gotten up from a nap, everything neat and my best nightgown, pink silk with lots of lace, from the most expensive lingerie store in Paris, on the sheets.

I saw that the tall man, whose name is William, but they call him Will, was late in coming back and I thought he would be looking at everything. Maybe she discovered my favorite dildo, inside a white cloth case in the bathroom.

In the meantime I was talking to the short guy, Jesse, who kept telling silly jokes that made me laugh.

The mojito had been enough to cheer me up. He approached me and wanted to remove my jacket, underneath I was only wearing a very low-cut black lace bra, but I let him.

When he left me in a bra he was quiet looking at me, very cut.

At that moment his friend appeared with two glasses in hand and also stood still.

"It's ok," I said.

And I began to open the buttons of the fat boy's shirt, who let himself be done, motionless.

The other came over, handed him the drink, and gulped down half the whiskey.

He moved to my other side and began to caress my back and neck.

I closed my eyes and leaned into his mouth, he kissed very well and he smelled rich, spices with lemon, the typical British aftershave.

His friend began to caress me by his side, but his hands went down to my chest and began to surround my hidden nipples behind the black lace.

I must have sighed with satisfaction, because a mouth kissed me on the lips and hands began to undress me.

She was wearing a skirt, a petticoat, a black thong and garter stockings, all prepared.

The skirt had no buttons and was removed only if I lifted my ass, and I did it lightly.

I kept the petticoat, which seemed to fascinate them.

These Americans don't know much about European sophistication, I thought, and watched as he caressed my thighs under the silk, his erections began to appear in his pants.

With my hands I caressed their penises and I noticed how they were surprised.

"Let's go to my room, it will be more comfortable," I murmured.

And I took them both by the hand.

At that moment I heard a slight noise, and I understood that you had already had time to enter the room with the second card, while we were drinking at the bar.

I knew you were hiding in the closet, getting ready to see.

It was a closet big enough that you could sit comfortably in a chair, leaning on my clothes, surrounded by my suits and my perfume, with the closet door ajar.

I know what you like to look at me and that you weren't uncomfortable, I left my favorite thong, the white one, out of the drawer.

Surely you have already started to masturbate with him slowly, as you like.

The gentlemen led me to bed, there was little lighting, two lighted candles and a lamp on the table covered by one of my silk handkerchiefs, which gave off a very pretty pink light.

They gently laid me down and began to caress me.

One licked my nipples over the bra, the other kissed my belly and began to lower his mouth over the petticoat.

Will, the tall friend, seeing how I did not move to undress them, took off his pants and then realized that he was still wearing his shoes, dear, like a newcomer, I thought.

But he managed to get naked in a minute.

I caught a glimpse of a thin but very long cock, a little crooked.

He got down on his knees beside me and I quickly caught his cock with my hand.

He grabbed it from me, apologized, and quickly put on a condom.

As soon as I saw her covered sex, I put it in my mouth.

I felt his start and that of his friend, who turned with his mouth open.

He took advantage of the fact that we were busy to undress him, just as quickly, and lie down next to me.

I noticed how with one of his hands he lifted my petticoat and with the other he took off the thong with flowers that matched my bra.

Then I noticed his breath on my pussy and how he began to lick my vulva carefully.

His friend Jesse meanwhile was about to come and was surprised to see how he did not remove his cock from my mouth.

He released so much semen that part of it splashed on me, it tasted sweet, with a light taste, without acidity.

I licked him some more and let him fall next to me, with a grateful smile.

Jesse continued licking and stroking my thighs and clit with his tongue, while Will, once recovered, began to caress my breasts.

When Jesse noticed me coming for the first time, he put on a rubber band in a second and lifted my legs and placed them on his shoulders.

Her sex penetrated me easily, but I was surprised by its thickness.

It wasn't as long as his friend's, but it was as if a tree stump had gently entered me.

He started ramming me while his friend continued to grab my breasts and lick my perky nipples with appetite.

He came in a moment, too fast I thought, but he didn't pull his penis out of my vulva.

He stood for a few minutes, as if recovering, and I didn't dare to move.

I just turned my face to the ajar closet and took the opportunity to kiss Will once more, and caress his torso.

It was not furry at all and although it was somewhat fat it was not flabby at all, but compact.

When I touched his chest I concentrated on his nipples, something that has an infallible effect in my experience, and I saw how his dick was getting hard again, no, very hard.

Meanwhile Jesse had gotten excited again and was penetrating me like a locomotive, he came right away again and carefully placed himself beside me, sweaty and very red.

This one should be allowed to rest, I thought, and turned to Will.

He lunged at me and started stroking and licking my neck and ears first, then down my breasts and my belly button and ended up in my shaved pussy.

He kept muttering things that he didn't understand, but I didn't care, he looked like a child in a toy store, he caressed my red and shiny vulva with his fingers, kissed it, licked it and carefully inserted two fingers inside my pussy.

He began to touch inside until he found the small relief of my G-spot and he caressed it very gently.

The good thing about North American lovers is that they are well educated by their very demanding females who do not settle for anything.

Technique they are phenomenal, they are clean and polite.

Imagination and hooliganism are qualities that they do not have in general ... but in this case I had two bodies at my disposal and my love watching from the ajar closet, surely masturbating with my soft thong, surrounded by my clothes and with my mouth ajar.

Finally I got up, had run again, and asked Will to lie on his back.

I stroked him too and gave him a rubber band.

As soon as I saw her placed, I literally sat on her sex and began to sit up looking at her face.

He grabbed onto my breasts and kneaded them like bread, then pulled on a pillow quadrant to bury his face in my tits, giving me light, non-marking bites.

I contracted my muscles attentively, and with my left hand began to caress his hairy balls that contracted on the spot.

I put one of my fingers in his mouth and then I placed it on the edge of his anus, a good fuck he needs, I thought, when I saw how his face changed.

Jesse had moved a little closer and with a light finger started to jerk me off.

When his fingers got wet, he got behind me and touched my ass.

Another anime ... I thought.

And I noticed how he began to caress my slit and put his fingers towards my pink asshole.

He put his fingers back in my pussy that was still occupied by Will's dick and slowly ran my asshole again.

He stuck one finger in, and when he saw that I didn't protest he put another in, patiently until my muscles relaxed.

Will pulled me, he wanted to lick my nipples to his liking and Jesse took the opportunity to kneel behind me and put it all the way.

I winced and froze.

But you can see that both of them had a lot of practice and one began to enter when the other was leaving, entering and leaving, leaving and entering, while I came closing my eyes, breathing through my mouth and feeling the ham of the sandwich ...

I heard the closet door open and glanced sideways as Jesse and Will continued in and out.

I saw the sparkle in your eyes and I thought: "My love, I dedicate it to you", and I continued to receive both penises until both friends came at the same time.

I couldn't take it anymore, I wanted them to leave my bed, my room and my life, but I didn't say anything.

I dropped down and closed my eyes as if I was dozing, and I saw how they went together to the bathroom, they must have fixed themselves and soon after they left the room after giving me a kiss on the hair.

I mumbled a thank you with my eyes closed and turned around.

Total, in a few hours, even if they look for me I will not be there, what does it matter ...

I heard the door close and stood still.

I heard your closet door open and I opened my eyes.

It was you with a look that burned and you sat next to me.

"My love, I really liked it. Now it's my turn."

I know you don't usually like or taste your cum when you cum in my mouth, but you surprise me once again.

You lean towards my sex, swollen and shiny, it has almost no semen because it did not come off the condoms, but I smell like sex and I am well fucked.

You bring your face close to my shell and start licking it first slowly and then quickly, I feel you are extremely excited.

I am what the English call a buttered bun, a freshly used pussy, and your sex is delighted to meet me.

You penetrate me quickly, you fuck me with passion, you bite my ear, you whisper in my ear ...

"Bitch, you're my bitch, other guys fuck you, but nobody gives you the pleasure that I give you, who do you think you are, you're mine" and you know that I come just from being in your arms and hearing you talk to me like that.

You come right away and as soon as you remove your cock you pick me up.

"Now to the bathroom."

I know what you want ... for me to stand in the bathroom and you between my knees, with my mouth open, waiting for me to give you a golden shower or for the semen and the cum that I have on my body to fall ... .

Only you like this show of trust and intimacy, only you whom I love, with whom I have the complicity of a hidden and lasting love.

You take me by the hand, you place me in the bathtub, you make hot water come out for my feet, in a few seconds it begins to come out of my shell with cum and mixed semen, you masturbate me slightly while you squeeze my belly that you kiss, I smell male I already sweat and I know you like it.

You keep squeezing my gut and jerking off until your golden shower comes out, you lick your lips, you sit up and you shower with me.

We lather slowly, we dry ourselves together, and both of us, clean and tired, lay down on the bed.

You cover me with affection and you say good night.

Tomorrow we will each go their own way, but thinking about the next meeting.

I love u

END

www.ingramcontent.com/pod-product-compliance
Lightning Source LLC
Chambersburg PA
CBHW051828130726
47987CB00003B/1451